by **Janet Lawler**

# Tyrannoclaus

illustrated by **John Shroades**

**HarperCollins**Publishers

Tyrannoclaus

Text copyright © 2009 by Janet Lawler

Illustrations copyright © 2009 by John Shroades

Manufactured in China.

Library of Congress Cataloging-in-Publication Data

Lawler, Janet.

    Tyrannoclaus / by Janet Lawler ; illustrated by John Shroades. — 1st ed.

        p.    cm.

    Summary: Disaster nearly prevents a dinosaur Santa Claus from delivering toys to
the prehistoric children on Christmas.

    ISBN 978-0-06-117054-6

    [1. Stories in rhyme. 2. Santa Claus—Fiction. 3. Dinosaurs—Fiction.]
I. Shroades, John, ill. II. Moore, Clement Clarke, 1779-1863. Night before
Christmas. III. Title.

PZ8.3.L355Iy 2009                    2008031456

[E]—dc22                          CIP

                                                 AC

Typography by Dana Fritts

09  10  11  12  13  SCP  10 9 8 7 6 5 4 3 2 1 ❖ First Edition

To Terry, Big T, and Barry
(my favorite T. rex)
—J.L.

To Connie, Jacob,
and Adam
—J.S.

'Twas the night before Christmas in dinosaur land.
Tyrannoclaus hurried, his helpers at hand.

They gathered up treats and created new toys
for stegosaur girls and apatosaur boys—
for the meat eaters, bones that were tasty to chew;
for plant eaters, leaves that were tender and new.

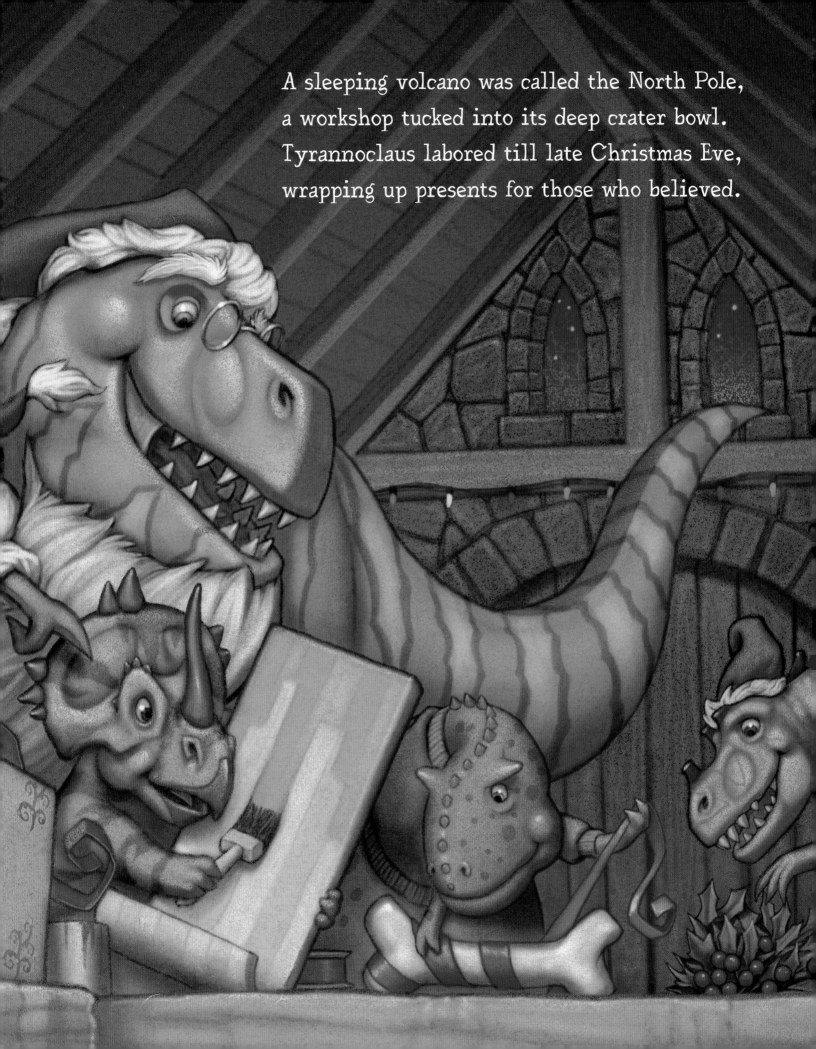

A sleeping volcano was called the North Pole,
a workshop tucked into its deep crater bowl.
Tyrannoclaus labored till late Christmas Eve,
wrapping up presents for those who believed.

But baby pteranodon wings were still flapping.
Tiny triceratops wouldn't start napping.
The swamps weren't sleepy, for no one could wait
for dear old Tyrannoclaus. Would he be late?

As dawn was approaching, the youngsters all snored.
While dreaming of goodies, they rumbled and roared.

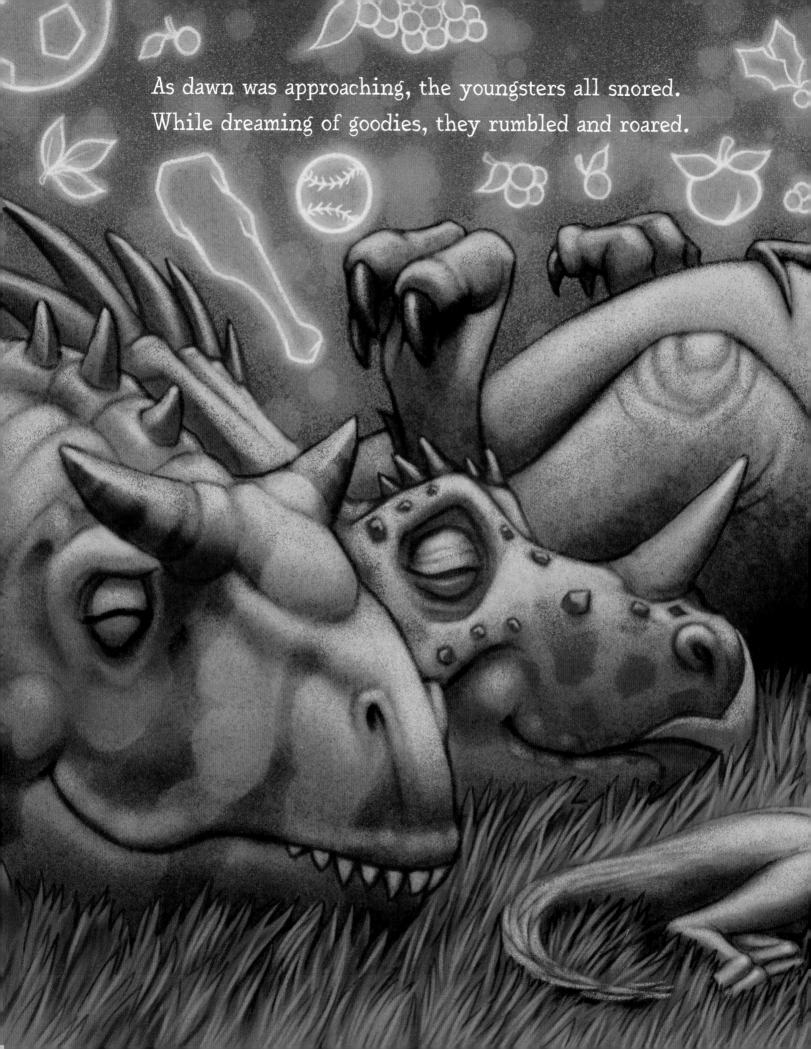

But back in the workshop, big trouble had started.
The sleigh was half empty. It should have departed.
Tyrannoclaus bellowed, "Where *can* my list be?
The dinosaur children are counting on me!"

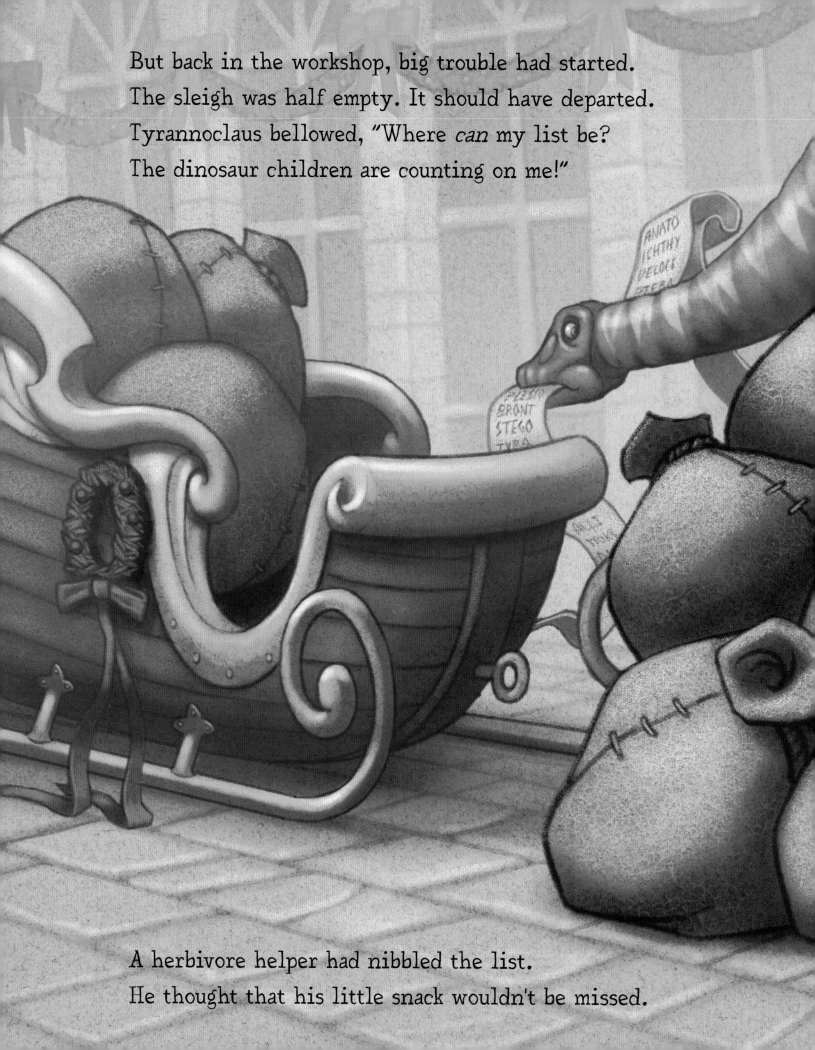

A herbivore helper had nibbled the list.
He thought that his little snack wouldn't be missed.

They taped up the pieces. The presents were packed.
But under the sleigh the earth trembled and cracked.

And three sacks of toys tumbled down off the side,
right into a crevice that split open wide.
By dropping a rescue rope made from a vine,
they pulled up the bags and the gifts were all fine.

"Quickly!" Tyrannoclaus cried. "Let's get going!"
Then off flew his hat—a hot breeze was now blowing.

One of his helpers swooped up in a flash and
dove down like a comet through thickening ash.

And just as Tyrannoclaus shouted, "Away!"
a blast rocked the ground and he tipped with the sleigh.

The mountain erupted! Tyrannoclaus stopped,
the sleigh stuck in lava that sizzled and popped.
His beard singed with embers, he tried to push off.
His eyes began stinging. He started to cough.

Tyrannoclaus yelled to his dinosaur team
to plunge through the fire, the smoke, and the steam.
"On Raptor! On Rexy! On Mimus and Saurus!
Oh, please pull us through all the dangers before us!"

They strained and they snorted while dripping with sweat,
to break from the lava before it could set.
With one final effort, at last they pulled free,
soared up past the crater, beyond every tree.

They circled the earth and they stopped at each nest,
delivering presents without any rest.

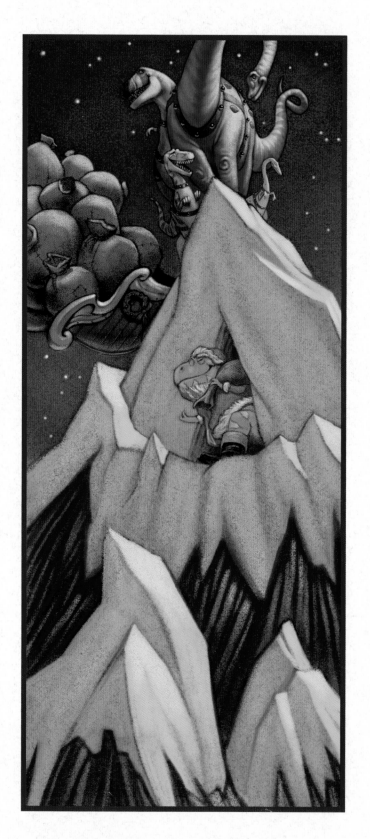

Tyrannoclaus wore a big smile on his face,
rushing to reach every dinosaur's place—
those high on a hilltop, those under a log,
those in between rocks in the back of a bog.

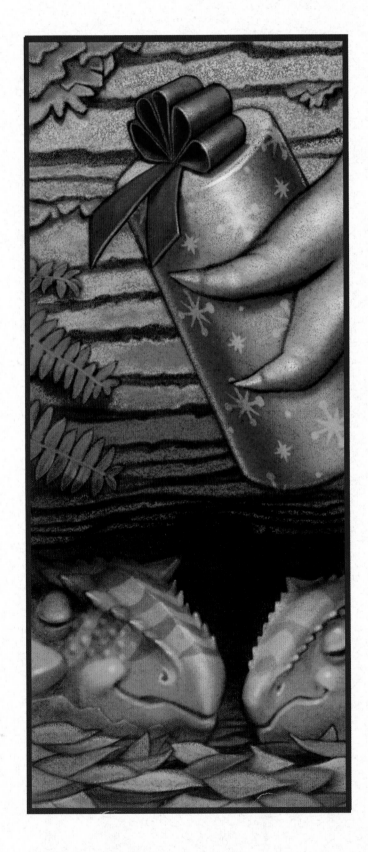

The toy sacks were empty as daylight appeared.
The sleigh headed north while Tyrannoclaus steered.

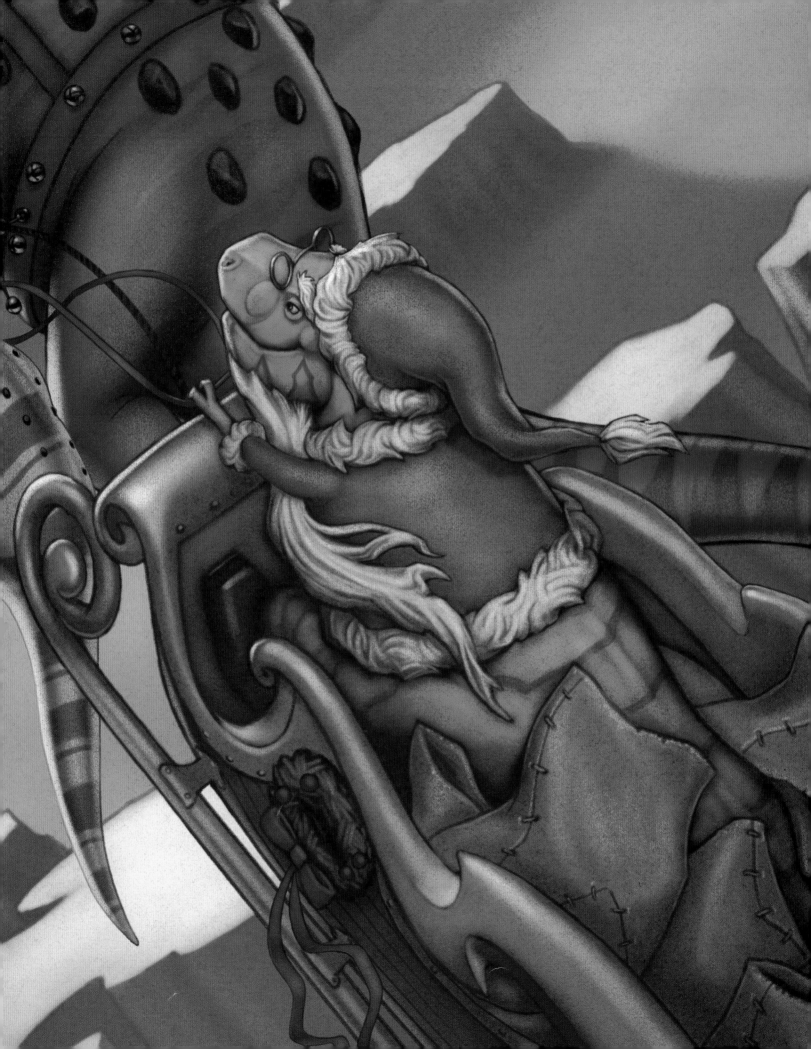

He called, "Merry Christmas!" and as he flew by,
he heard "Oohs!" and "Aahs!" floating up through the sky
from dinosaur children, so happy below,
so giddy and gleeful, with eyes all aglow.

They picked up their treasures and ran out to play
on Christmas, the very best dinosaur day!